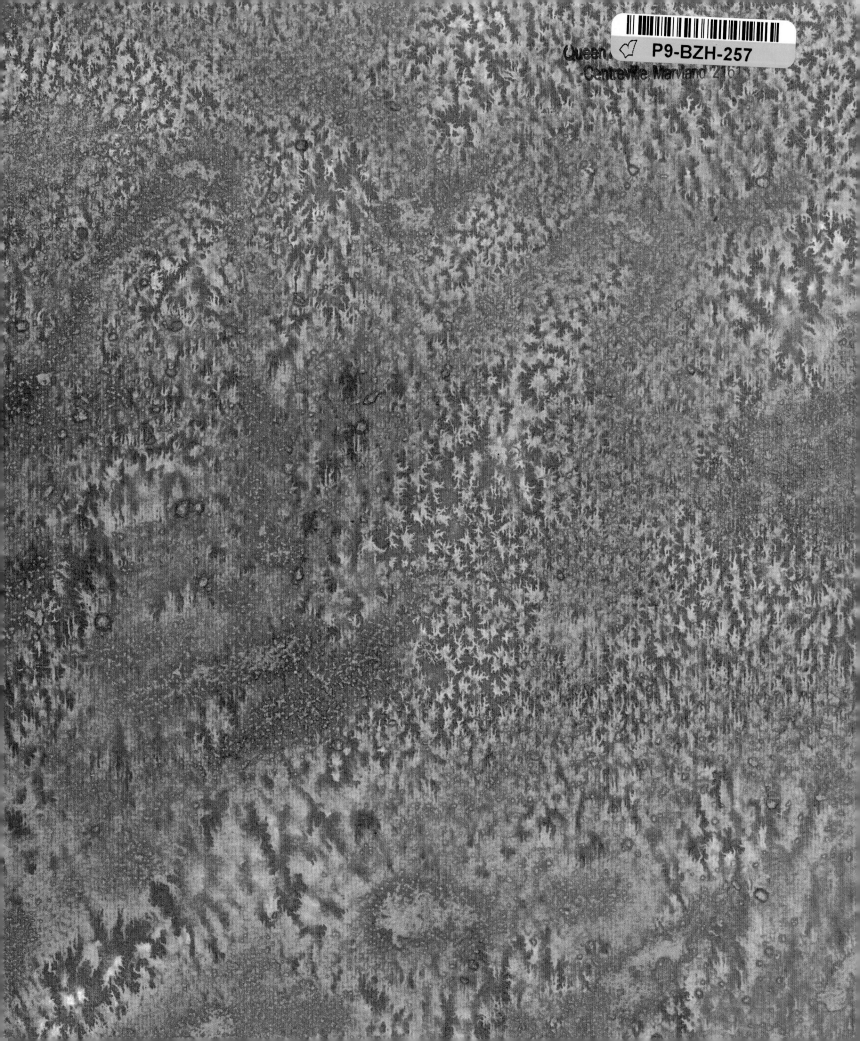

For Osky Bosky Boy (Oscar) — *M.P.R.*

BWI   15.99   1/06

Published in the United States 2001 by Phyllis Fogelman Books
An imprint of Penguin Putnam Books for Young Readers
345 Hudson Street, New York, New York 10014

Published in Great Britain 2000 by Frances Lincoln Limited,
4 Torriano Mews, Torriano Avenue, London NW5 2RZ
Copyright © 2000 by M. P. Robertson

Printed in Hong Kong
7 9 8

The
EGG

M. P. Robertson

PHYLLIS FOGELMAN BOOKS

NEW YORK

George knew something wasn't right when he found more than he had bargained for under his mother's favorite chicken.

He moved the egg to the warmth
of his bedroom. For three days
and three nights he read the egg stories.

On the third night the egg started to rumble.

Something was hatching, and it definitely wasn't a chicken!

When the dragon saw George, it gave a chirrup of delight.

George didn't speak Dragon, but he knew exactly what the dragon had said:
"Mommy."

George had never been a mother before, but he knew that it was his motherly duty to teach the dragon dragony ways.

The first lesson he taught was *The Fine Art of Flying.*

The second lesson was *Fire and How to Breathe It.*

The third lesson was *How to Distress a Damsel*.

And the final lesson was *How to Defeat a Knight*.

Every evening, as all good
mothers should, George
read the dragon a bedtime
story.

One night, as he read
from a book of dragon
tales, the dragon looked
longingly at the pictures.
A sizzling tear rolled down
his scaly cheek.

The dragon was lonely.
He was missing his own kind.

The next morning the dragon had gone.
George was very sad. He thought he
would never see his dragon again.

But seven nights later he was woken
by the beating of wings. Excitedly
he pulled back the curtains. There, perched in
the tree, was the dragon. George opened
the window and clambered onto his back.

They soared into the night, chasing the moon around the world, over oceans and mountains and cities.

Faster and faster they went, until they came to a place that was neither North nor South, East nor West.

They swooped down through the clouds into a cave that gaped like a dragon's jaws. This was the place where dragons lived.

The dragon gave a roar of delight. He was home at last.

Finally it was time for George to leave.
Up, up they flew, chasing sleep through the night,
until they could see his home below.

George hugged his dragon tight, and the dragon gave a roar. George didn't speak Dragon, but he knew exactly what the dragon had said:

"Thank you."

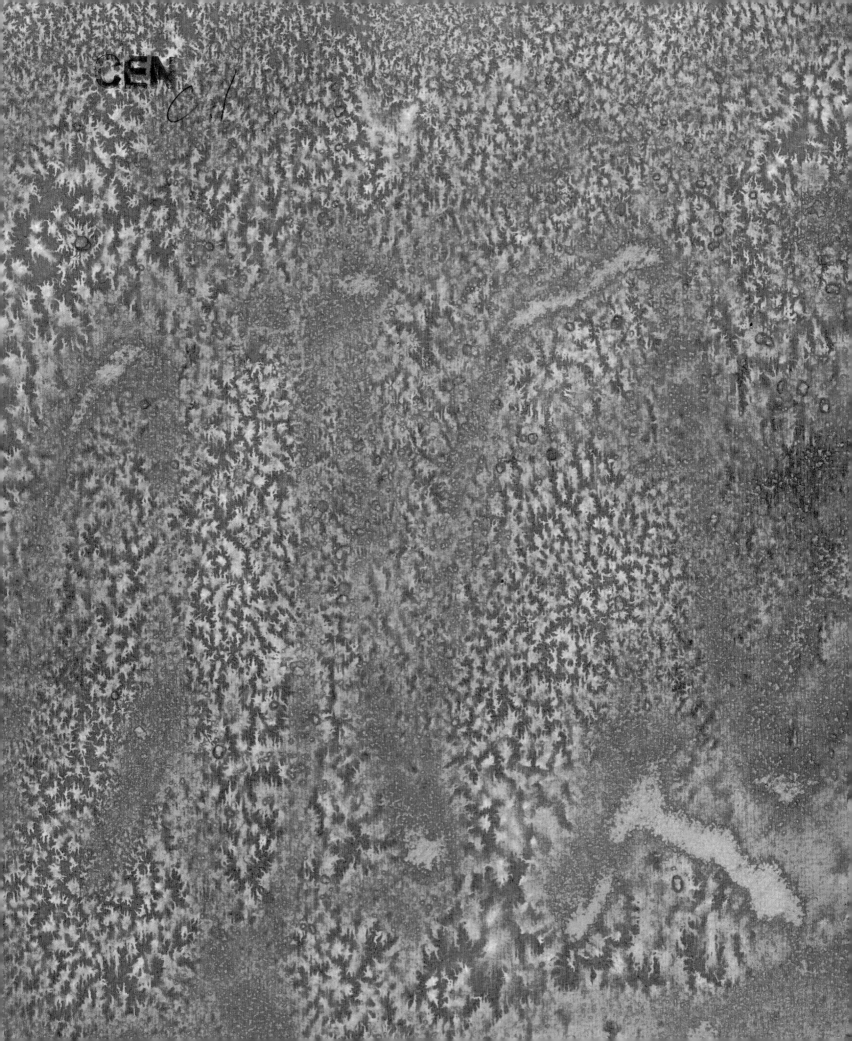